MAR - 2008

8 /.00

W9-BGK-321

THIS CANDLEWICK BOOK BELONGS TO:

_____

_____

_____

For Kate and Fred

First U.S. edition 2007

Library of Congress Cataloging-in-Publication Data is available.

Library of Congress Catalog Card Number pending

ISBN 978-0-7636-3570-1

2 4 6 8 10 9 7 5 3 1

Printed in China

This book was typeset in Optima.
The illustrations were done in colored pencil.

Candlewick Press
2067 Massachusetts Avenue
Cambridge, Massachusetts 02140

visit us at www.candlewick.com

Jane
and the
DRAGON

Martin Baynton

CANDLEWICK PRESS
CAMBRIDGE, MASSACHUSETTS

Jane hated sewing. Every morning she sat with her
mother practising her stitches, and every morning she
gazed down at the knights practising their swordplay
in the courtyard below.

Jane longed to be a knight. Nothing else would do, and she told her mother so.

Her mother laughed.

"Such foolishness," she said. "You will be a lady-in-waiting. Perhaps, like me, you will become lady-in-waiting to the Queen herself."

Jane was very upset. But she was determined to be a knight and she went to tell her father.

Her father laughed.

"What nonsense," he said. "Only boys can become knights."

Jane told the King.
The King laughed.
"Of course, of course,"
he said. But he hadn't
really heard her, for
the King listened to
no one but himself.

Jane told the Prince, the King's only son.
The Prince said nothing. He just
laughed and pushed her over
in the royal sandpit.

Jane told the knights themselves. They laughed and dressed her in fine armour that was too big for her and set her on a straw horse.

They thought it was great fun until they saw tears trickle out from under the helmet. The knights were sorry. They had not meant to be unkind.

Finally Jane told the court jester. The jester didn't laugh. Of all the people Jane had spoken to, he alone listened and understood.

He took Jane to his room and opened a wooden chest. Inside was a small suit of armour.

"I wanted to be a knight as well," said the jester, "but I was too small. This armour is my secret; I put it on sometimes . . . and dream a little. I want you to have it."

Jane was overjoyed.

"But what about your dream?" she asked.

"I was never really brave enough," he said. "You dream it for me."

From that day on, Jane's sewing got worse. She was too busy watching the knights – watching and learning.

And whenever the knights were out chasing the King's enemies, Jane would go to their quarters, put on her armour and practise.

She practised her swordplay.

She practised her horseplay.

She even practised
her victory speeches.

Then one terrible day, an enormous green dragon came and stole the Prince.

The King and Queen were horrified. They called for the knights, but the knights were away at a jousting carnival.

"Is there no one left who can save our son?" cried the King.

They were very surprised when a small knight ran into the courtyard, saddled up the Prince's pony and galloped away after the dragon.

Jane followed the dragon to his mountain lair.

"Release the boy!" she demanded in her sternest voice.

The dragon laughed.

"Make me!" he roared, and his hot breath singed the plume on Jane's helmet.

Jane drew her sword and advanced. A long and dreadful battle followed. Twice Jane could have stabbed the dragon, but she did not. Twice the dragon could have toasted her with his hot breath, but he did not.

At last they were too exhausted to fight on, and they sat down together on the floor of the cave.

"You could have killed me," said the dragon.

"You could have killed me," said Jane. "Why didn't you?"

"I don't like hurting people," sighed the dragon.

"Then why did you steal the Prince?"

"Because it's expected of me."

"Then do the unexpected," said Jane.

"No, no! I couldn't. I'm not . . . brave enough."

"Of course you are. It's easy."

"Easy for you," said the dragon, "you're a knight and people expect you to be brave."

Jane laughed and took off her helmet. The dragon was amazed.

"You're just a girl, I could fry you for breakfast."

"Yes, that would be easy for you. It would be easy for me to be a lady-in-waiting, people expect it. But I want to be a knight. What do you want?"

"I want to be loved," sobbed the dragon, and he covered his face with a spiky brown wing.

Jane put down her sword and kissed him. "I love you," she said.

"Oh, thank you, thank you," said the dragon, and he sobbed all the louder.

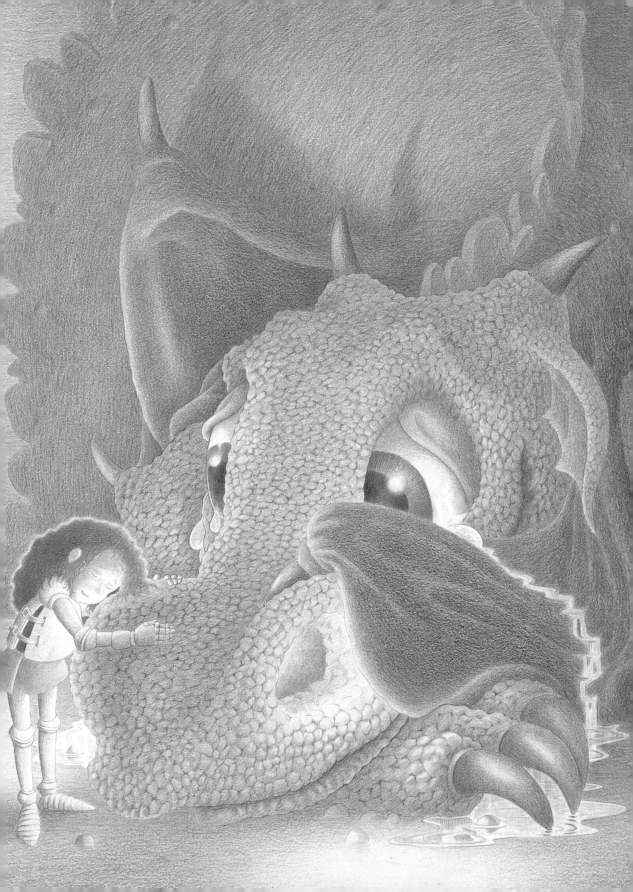

"Now I have to take the Prince home," said Jane. "The King and Queen will be dreadfully worried."

"Will you visit me sometimes?" asked the dragon.

"Every Saturday," Jane promised. "But now we really must go."

And she gave the dragon a hug and another kiss.

It was late in the day when they arrived back at the castle. The entire court rushed out to greet them. The King and Queen were overjoyed to see their son – but who was the mysterious knight?

Jane took off her helmet, and the crowd gasped.

Her father just stood there with his mouth wide open. Her mother fainted gracefully.

"Dear Jane," said the King, "how can we ever thank you?"

"Your Majesty, I would like to become a proper knight please, with every Saturday off to visit a friend."

"Certainly, certainly," said the King, and he called for the royal scribe, who wrote the contract out there and then.

That evening the King gave a royal ball. Everyone was there, including Jane's mother and father, who had recovered from their shock and were now very proud of their fearless daughter.

Jane was the guest of honour.

"You must choose a partner, Jane," said the King, "and lead the dancing."

All the handsome young men waited, each one hoping to be chosen.

But Jane took the jester's hand and led him onto the floor.

"Thank you for the armour," said Jane.

"Thank you for the dream," said the jester.

And together they danced and danced and danced.

About the author...

Martin Baynton wanted to reverse the traditional treatment of fairytale heroines with this story. He says, "Fairy tales are tough on girls. Within their cruel pages, girls scrub floors, eat poisoned apples, sleep for centuries and are only saved when a handsome prince arrives to sweep them off their blistered knees into a world of Happily Ever After. Not so Jane. Jane saves herself and she most definitely does not want to live happily ever after. She wants adventure, danger, challenge – and 'happy' just isn't enough."

Martin has been a writer and illustrator since 1980 and has an international reputation for his books for children. He has recently partnered with the Academy award-winning Weta Workshop (The Lord of the Rings trilogy) and the Canadian children's television producers, Nelvana, to create a stunning animated television series based on the books, using the latest digital effects technology.

As well as writing and illustrating picture books for children, Martin also writes for the stage, television, film and radio. He was born in the UK and now lives in New Zealand.